P9-ELD-819

First American Edition 1996 by Kane/Miller Book Publishers
Brooklyn, New York & La Jolla, California

Originally published in Spanish under the title *Niña Bonita*
by Ediciones Ekaré, Caracas, Venezuela
(The Portuguese version, titled *Menina Bonita* by Ana Maria Machado
first published in Brazil)

Copyright © 1994 Ediciones Ekaré
American text copyright © 1996 Kane/Miller Book Publishers
All rights reserved.

First American Paperback Edition 2001

For information contact
Kane/Miller Book Publishers
P.O. Box 310529, Brooklyn, N.Y. 11231-0529

Library of Congress Catalog Card Number 95-81577
ISBN 1-929132-11-5

Printed and bound in Singapore by Tien Wah Press Pte, Ltd.
1 2 3 4 5 6 7 8 9 10

NINA BONITA

A Story by Ana Maria Machado
Illustrated by Rosana Faría
Translated from Spanish by Elena Iribarren

A CRANKY NELL BOOK

KM Kane/Miller Book Publishers

Brooklyn, New York & La Jolla, California

There once lived a little girl who was called Nina Bonita. Her eyes were like two shiny black olives. Her hair was curly and pitch black, as if made of unwoven threads of the night. Her skin was dark and glossy, just like a panther in the rain.

Her mother loved to comb her hair and would sometimes make tiny braids tied with colored ribbons. Then Nina Bonita would look just like a princess from the Continent of Africa or a fairy from the Kingdom of the Moon.

Next door to her house lived a white rabbit with pink ears, deep red eyes and a quivering nose. The rabbit thought that Nina Bonita was the loveliest person he had ever seen, and he said with a sigh, "When I get married, I would like to have a daughter as black and as pretty as she."

One day he went to her house and asked, "Little girl, little girl, tell me your secret. What makes your skin so dark and so pretty?"

Nina Bonita didn't know, but she made something up. "Oh, I guess when I was a baby, some black ink spilled on me."

The rabbit found a bottle of black ink and poured it all over himself. He turned black and was very pleased. But just then a rain shower washed away the ink, and the rabbit became white again.

He returned to Nina Bonita's house and asked again, "Little girl, little girl, tell me your secret. What makes your skin so dark and so pretty?"

Nina Bonita didn't know, but again she made something up. "Ah, I guess when I was a baby, I drank lots of black coffee."

The rabbit went back home. He drank so much coffee that he couldn't sleep a wink and spent the whole night going to the bathroom. What's more, he didn't turn black.

Again he went to Nina Bonita's house and asked, "Little girl, little girl, tell me your secret. What makes your skin so dark and so pretty?"

Nina Bonita didn't know, but she made something up. "Er, I guess when I was a baby, I ate lots of blackberries."

The rabbit bought a basket of blackberries. He ate and ate until he was so stuffed he could hardly move. His belly ached, and again he spent the whole night going to the bathroom. Still, he didn't turn black.

When he felt better, he went back to Nina Bonita and asked once again, "Little girl, little girl, tell me your secret. What makes your skin so dark and so pretty?"

Nina Bonita didn't know and was about to make up yet another story about some black beans. But her mother overheard and decided it was time to set things straight. "What secret? Why, she looks just like her black grandmother."

The rabbit, who was silly, but not as silly as he may have seemed, realized that Nina Bonita's mother must be telling the truth. After all, people usually look like their parents and grandparents, uncles and aunts, and even their distant relatives. So if he wanted to have a daughter as black and as pretty as Nina Bonita, he would have to find the right rabbit to marry.

He didn't have to look very far. Soon enough he
met a nice female rabbit who was as black as the night,
and who thought the white rabbit was quite charming.
They fell in love, got married and started having bunnies,
lots of them, because when rabbits start having babies,
they never seem to stop.

They had bunnies of every color and shade: white bunnies, gray bunnies, half white–half gray bunnies, white bunnies with black spots, black bunnies with white spots, and one very pretty bunny with very black fur.

Naturally, Nina Bonita became the black bunny's godmother.

Whenever the bunny went out for a stroll, someone would ask, "Little bunny, little bunny, tell me your secret. What makes your fur so black and so pretty?"

And she would answer, "I look just like my mother. *That's* our secret."